MILLIONS OF LITTLE THREADS

BY ROBERT PANTANO
of Pursuit of Wonder

Copyright © 2023 by Robert Pantano

All rights reserved. No part of this publication may be reproduced, distributed, or transmitted in any form or by any means, including photocopying, recording, or other electronic or mechanical methods, without permission in writing from the publisher, except in the case of brief quotes used in reviews and other non-commercial purposes permitted by copyright law.

The characters and events in this book are fictitious. Any apparent similarities to actual persons or events, living or dead, past or present, are not intended by the author and are entirely coincidental.

A Pursuit of Wonder publication.

CONTENTS

Chapter 1: Implantation 1
Chapter 2: Reconciliation 13
Chapter 3: Incomprehension 17
Chapter 4: Rehabilitation 33
Chapter 5: Disconsolation 41

About the Author 51

CHAPTER 1: IMPLANTATION

Kennedy had waited three months for this day. October 18th, 2062: the day of his appointment. He was about to receive the latest version of the Lerna Inc. brain-machine interface—his first BMI. He was eager and ready to join the rest of the world in this new realm of technology and thought and being, where everything would be even faster, easier, better.

Like many others, Kennedy had held off on buying a brain-machine interface for a while after they had become publicly available. Initially, BMIs were only for individuals who needed them for a fairly specific reason. Individuals who suffered from body paralysis could use them to regain function of their limbs or control mechanical prosthetics. Cognitively impaired patients could restore their learning faculties or improve their memory. And servicemembers, like special operations forces, could interact with machines and devices in high-stakes situations more efficiently and hands-free. Soon, however, BMIs became available to the general public, and soon, the average person began to adopt the technology.

The more normal it became, the more people felt the need to adopt it. And the more people who adopted it,

Chapter 1: Implantation

the more normal it became, until finally, it became abnormal to not have one. And most people do not want to be strange and abnormal—or worse, left out. And most people are willing to sacrifice almost anything, including themselves, to ensure that they are not.

Three months prior to his appointment, Kennedy was at a work event. He worked in finance as a junior analyst at Praxis, a major multinational crypto management and financial services company. Being just twenty-one years old, this was quite the opportunity.

Every year, Praxis held a mandatory in-person, company-wide conference. This was the second one Kennedy had attended. Unlike the first one, however, this time, essentially all of his co-workers were using BMIs. He observed employees communicating with each other via their thoughts alone, sharing information by transmitting thoughts as text and audio messages, and interacting with the conference space hands-free and without any other physical devices. It was completely surreal seeing BMIs used so universally in one place for the first time.

During part of the event, Kennedy sat in the main conference hall with his co-worker and best friend John while various company executives and directors gave presentations. During one of the presentations given by a director Kennedy and John worked under, the director said, "Being in crypto management means you need the newest and most advanced technologies. It's that simple. You need to be able to efficiently communicate with others in the industry, track the world's systems and events, use industry-leading standards and software, and of course, you need to not seem like an idiot—someone who's normal, adept, up to speed with the latest tech. Who's going to trust you with their digital assets if you're still working with one of these?"

The director held up a handtop computer, the most commonly used device prior to BMIs. It's what Kennedy still used.

After the event concluded, Kennedy walked to the hyperloop station with John. Kennedy had become really close with John, who was around the same age as him and had started working at Praxis around the same time. He was one of Kennedy's only friends.

"You really need to get one at this point, man. I think you're one of the only people I know who doesn't have one," John said.

"I know. I already decided. I'm scheduling my appointment tonight."

"Fuck yeah, man. Good. The procedure is honestly no worse than a teeth cleaning, and I'm telling you it doesn't feel weird at all. It's literally the best thing I've ever bought. It's like another form of existence. I can't even really describe it. Imagine thinking your own thoughts and doing everything normally, but everything you need and want is like right there, always synced with you."

The two arrived at the hyperloop station.

"I'm literally bored all the time, so even just for that reason alone, I'm convinced," Kennedy said.

The two laughed.

"Alright, I'll see you tomorrow, man," Kennedy continued.

"Yeah, see you tomorrow, man. Good luck with setting everything up."

Chapter 1: Implantation

The two bumped fists and then went different directions.

Kennedy arrived at his apartment—a minimalistic one-bedroom with light beige oak wooden floors and quartz countertops. In the living room, there was a small, white loveseat, a VR treadmill, and a lamp. Outside of work, Kennedy spent most of his time here, alone, streaming videos or reading books on his couch or playing video games and exercising on his VR treadmill. He spent a good amount of time watching and reading content about finance, economics, politics, and philosophy. He had a genuinely deep interest in these subjects and had big dreams of becoming a major cryptocurrency hedge fund manager, and he wanted to understand all the in-and-outs of things related to this goal. Kennedy had unknowingly inherited a deep desire to become wealthy and important from his father, a successful businessman who always prioritized money and status, and often psychologically beat on Kennedy and his brother Max to mold the same values into them.

Tonight, however, Kennedy sat on his couch and scheduled an appointment for a BMI implantation.

Lerna Inc. was by far the most popular BMI company. It had forged itself through the fires of aggressive competition amongst other BMI hardware companies throughout the 2040s. It emerged not only with ownership over the majority of the BMI market but also with massive influence over the state of the world in general—everything from collective culture to individual lives. Lerna released a new BMI model every year or so, and whenever they did, millions of people around the world waited on the Lerna website, hoping to be some of the first in line to order. Since implanting the device required a procedure that took about an hour, there were only so many slots available at any given time, and so, there was always a long waitlist, adding an air of urgency and significance to the process and further fueling the demand.

On his handtop computer, Kennedy went to the Lerna website and purchased the latest available BMI model. He then created a Lerna ID. The Lerna ID would contain his personal information associated with his government-issued identification, which would then all become assigned to his BMI. This would be crucial to everything. He would need his Lerna ID to access his BMI operating system, save and access his memory files, interface with applications, communicate with other BMI users, authenticate associated third-party accounts, and confirm his identity in general.

The latest BMI model cost $17,799 with free implantation—a reasonably affordable price. After purchasing it and creating an account, Kennedy digitally consented to all waivers and disclosed any medical conditions. Finally, he selected his ideal appointment dates at his ideal Lerna facility locations. The website then scheduled him at the earliest available slot.

Now, three months later, Kennedy sat in a hyperloop pod on his way to the Lerna facility.

He arrived at a long, narrow building with rounded corners, like a rounded-off half-cylinder. It had windows spanning the entire front side, which revealed a large, barren, open-concept lobby.

Once inside, Kennedy observed holographic displays of beautiful abstract photos and paintings, each stamped

Chapter 1: Implantation

with the Lerna logo—a simple, squiggly line that kind of resembled a capital L. One display had an image of a middle-aged woman who Kennedy recognized as the CEO. She looked cold and kind of distant. Her expression appeared like she was almost rehearsing being happy and friendly. There were also tables and cases scattered around the lobby with various models of brain-machine interfaces—as well as supplementary products and accessories. At the front, there were people sitting in widely spread-out chairs. In front of them were dark, metallic obelisks.

Kennedy approached one of the obelisks.

"Kennedy Weatherly. 2 p.m.," he said while activating the outward-facing display on his AR contact lenses, projecting his government-issued ID and his appointment QR code.

The obelisk scanned Kennedy's face and codes, confirming his identity and appointment. It then instructed him to wait in the lobby until he was called.

Kennedy sat while an automated voice called out names over the lobby's speaker system. While he waited, he used an AR application that allowed him to watch the real-time perspective of other people who livestreamed their lives and sold their decisions and actions to their audience. He watched one of his favorite streamers, named Peako, who often did man-on-the-street stuff, asking random people questions and doing absurd things in public spaces. Kennedy found him completely obnoxious, but there was something about watching another person's madness that made him feel saner. He did this for several hours and still had not yet been called. He could've sworn he had gotten there before several of the other people who had been called in.

As Kennedy was beginning to think something was wrong, the automated voice said, "Now serving Kennedy Weatherly in room #103."

Kennedy quickly jumped up, exhaling with relief.

Two doors opened at the front of the lobby, next to where he scanned in.

Once inside, Kennedy walked down a long corridor. Sleek metal doors lined both sides of the hall. He read the room numbers as he passed by them. It felt like the hall went on forever. When Kennedy finally approached a door that read *#103*, it opened automatically. He poked his head inside. There was no one—just a surgical chair in the middle of the room, two white bionic arms that looked like prosthetic human arms, and several other pieces of sleek machinery.

"Please confirm your identity by stating your name and displaying your ID," an automated voice said.

Kennedy did as he was instructed, and the door closed behind him.

"Thank you. You may take a seat, Kennedy," the voice continued.

Kennedy sat in the surgical chair. A red light on the side of the chair turned green. One of the robotic arms moved toward him and handed him a small metal cup containing three pills.

"Please swallow all three tablets. These are conscious sedation tablets. They will help you relax and block any pain during the procedure."

Chapter 1: Implantation

Kennedy took the cup, and the robotic arm retrieved a small bottle of water and handed it to him.

"Please confirm once you have taken the tablets."

Kennedy swallowed them.

"I have taken the tablets," Kennedy said.

The chair reclined and raised up slightly. A minute passed, and nothing happened. Then, Kennedy began to feel a soothing surge of bliss swell up from his chest and wash over his body. The world outside of him dissolved away along with his sense of self. Everything felt good. He felt an intimation of hope for what could be. He softly smiled, and his eyes rolled back.

"Please keep your head straight and stay as still as possible," the voice said.

A helmet-like, half-dome-shaped device moved onto Kennedy's head. It began scanning his brain while simultaneously drilling a small hole into his skull. Once a small dime-sized hole had been drilled, the machine discarded the piece of his skull and began implanting hundreds of tiny threads, each with hundreds of independent electrode arrays, connecting hundreds of thousands of electrodes to neurons throughout Kennedy's brain. It then implanted the Lerna BMI device into the hole, which was connected to all the threads on the other side. Finally, it coated over and sealed the device in with a skin-like super glue.

"Please remain in your seat until further instructions. It should take around thirty minutes for the sedation tablets to wear off."

Kennedy felt a slight pain in his head, but it was mild and offset by his growing excitement and anticipation.

After thirty minutes passed, the chair returned to its upright position.

"Congratulations. You are now fully integrated. You can activate your BMI by holding down the button on the top of your device for three seconds. Before exiting, please be sure to take your Lerna BMI 6S package with you, which contains your instruction manual and wireless charging port. Please note that you must be within twenty feet of your port to ensure reliable charging speed. If you experience any issues or complications, please visit Lerna Support for additional assistance."

A brief silence filled the room.

"Thank you, and have a wonderful day."

Kennedy got up, grabbed the small circular box on a stand over by the door, and then left back down the hallway.

He arrived back at his apartment. Once inside, he sat on his couch, paused for a moment, and then, held down the button on top of his head. A heads-up display screen appeared in front of him. But it wasn't in front of him. It was inside his head.

The BMI was actively processing and stimulating Kennedy's nerve impulses. In his visual cortex, sequences were activated to produce what appeared to be a regular visual perception of a holographic screen.

A blank, white screen read: *Hello.* Kennedy thought about wanting to change to the next screen, and the screen changed. The following screens asked him various questions and requested certain account information. Each time, as soon he read and understood the question and then indicated conscious intention to answer, the

Chapter 1: Implantation

device knew his answer and automatically moved on to the next screen. Finally, Kennedy mentally signed in to his Lerna ID, which setup and associated it with a Brain ID. The Brain ID was like a mental fingerprint, where the BMI scanned and mapped the specific structure of the user's brain and then locked the user and the user's Lerna ID to their specific BMI and their BMI to their brain. This was crucial because it was the only way to access your BMI with your Lerna ID once it was set up.

Once the set-up process was complete, a home screen appeared with a collection of built-in applications. Kennedy saw an app called Lerna Store. He wanted to open it, and it opened. The heads-up display screen showed a browser full of colorful icons. He spent hours sitting on his couch exploring all the available applications, looking at the previews, trying the trials, and downloading what he wanted.

First, he tried an app called Birdie, which allowed him to transcribe his thoughts, feelings, and memories into text, audio, and video messages, or create a copy of a literal mapping of his brain's current electrochemical state, which he could then post and transmit to other people with whom he was connected with on the app. Immediately, he connected with John, his brother, a couple other co-workers, and some old friends whom he still kept in loose contact with. Then, he copied and posted the experience of his current excitement.

Next, he tried an app called Swap, which was an experiential simulation app that provided a partial simulation of other people's, often famous people's, senses of self and experiences of daily life, updated in real-time based on the Swapper's brain state, which was scanned and transmitted out to their audience along with video footage. Kennedy looked through the top profiles. He found Peako, who had already formed a large Swapper following. Kennedy tried his. It was strange and kind of disorienting, but extremely fascinating and immersive. Kennedy's own world and life dissolved away for those moments as he peered into this other person's.

Finally, he downloaded Phaneron, an app that allowed him to upload, save, retrieve, and send memories and perceptions as files. It also allowed him to overlay and alter his real-time perceptions to contort to different realities and locations.

The whole thing was utterly surreal. Everything he had needed his hands for, his mouth for, his ears for; everything he had needed other devices for, his handtop computer, his smart contacts, his smart rings, his smart earpods, and nearly everything else, was now all integrated into him. He could perceive and interface with the entire Internet, digital applications, physical devices, other people, and essentially the whole world all through his mind alone. It was as if Kennedy was suddenly both telepathic and superconscious.

Although the whole experience of controlling a device with his thoughts alone was weird at first, after only a few hours or so, Kennedy quickly became used to it. It was completely intuitive, and he soon found that mentally deciding to type, scroll, zoom, or tap verses mentally deciding to type, scroll, zoom, or tap and then watching your arm and hand do it were fundamentally no different. It was much easier to just skip the extra steps.

Chapter 1: Implantation

Kennedy felt like he was being reborn into a new world with endless possibilities. Everything was infinitely easier, more integrated, more captivating.

CHAPTER 2: RECONCILIATION

Kennedy went to the coworking office space that he worked from in downtown. While on his morning commute on a hyperloop pod, he looked out at the city around him. Using a BMI app, he enhanced his perception, modifying the scent of the pod and the hue of the city. He connected and interfaced with the pod, slightly reclining his chair without physically doing anything. He read and sent a couple work messages by merely recording, editing, and sharing a couple thoughts through BMS messaging.

Kennedy arrived and walked into the large office space, passing by fake trees and plants, colorful glass pods, sleek cotton couches, and uniquely shaped wooden desks and chairs. As Kennedy approached his workstation, John turned in his chair toward him.

"So?" John said, pausing for a brief moment. "Crazy, right?!"

"Yeah, this shit is insane!" Kennedy said as he sat down next to him.

"I can't believe we've gone this long in life without this," John said.

"I know. I feel like a fucking legitimate android."

Chapter 2: Reconciliation

"So, what have you downloaded so far?" John asked.

Kennedy mentally scanned through his display screen.

"Overlay, Birdie, Alexia, MyPal, NueroTube, Helix, Phaneron, MindBook, Tinge … stuff like that."

"Okay. Yeah, I have most of those. Those are definitely good. Birdie is wild. How about Epoché? Did you get that one yet?"

"No. I've heard of it, though. Is it worth getting?"

"Yeah, I just got it pretty recently. I was kind of skeptical of a lot of those emotional network apps at first, but this one is actually pretty good. I definitely recommend it."

"What does it do? Just like monitor your emotions and help you track things?"

"Yeah, sort of. But it does a lot more than that. You can also interface back and forth with it, and it helps you regulate how you want to feel. It's hard to explain. Just try it," John replied.

"Okay, cool. Yeah, I definitely will. I'll download it on my break."

The two paused, intuitively understanding that they were going to begin working now. They turned their heads slightly away from each other, activating their display screens and overlaying a set of applications on the various glass panels extruding from their workstations.

Working with the BMI was incredible. It made everything easier and more succinct. Kennedy already had mental notifications setup for every time something noteworthy happened in the market. He had memory files saved and scheduling applications setup to help him remember what and when he needed to do things. He had begun applying different mental weightings to different tasks based on their level of priority. And of course, he could now communicate and execute work more efficiently by simply thinking about what he wanted to do, type, and send, and then, having it happen.

After working for a little while, Kennedy stopped to take a break. He was exhausted, and work was stressing him out. He was helping review a new larger client's portfolio, which was a significant opportunity for someone in his position, but also immensely stressful and high-pressure. He went over to the Lerna App Store and searched Epoché. He tapped on it. It had a 4.7-star rating from 2.4 million reviews. It was ranked number one in the *Emotional and Mental Wellbeing* category. At the top of the listing, text read: *What's New.* Underneath, text read: *The latest version contains bug fixes and performance improvements.* Below that was a description that read: *Distributes feedback signals into relevant parts of the brain to trigger neurotransmitters and provide sensations of pleasure, calm, euphoria, tiredness, focus, and more. Dampen brain activity that is causing negative conscious experiences, and enhance brain activity that causes positive experiences, increasing overall mood and quality of life. Feel how you want whenever you want.*

Kennedy looked at the preview screens of the app. It looked incredible—bright colors, beautiful imagery, clear and pleasing displays with wonderful UI design. It looked like candy. He downloaded it. As soon as he did, the app startup screen asked Kennedy to grant the app access to his Lerna ID and BMI, which he did. Then, it asked if he would like to allow Epoché to provide mental notifications. These things were essentially required for the app

Chapter 2: Reconciliation

to do its job, and so, Kennedy agreed to and accepted them all.

Immediately, Epoché began scanning Kennedy's brain, and a notification appeared. It read: *Low mood detected. Apply a mild mood booster for subtle but effective enhancement?* Kennedy tapped *Accept*, and then, the app stimulated specific neurons to send out dopamine neurotransmitters, which incited pleasant sensations and thoughts. He felt noticeably better right away.

CHAPTER 3: INCOMPREHENSION

A little over a year went by. It was a Tuesday, and Kennedy sat on the pod on his way home from work. The novelty of the BMI had mostly worn off, and it was now just an ordinary part of his everyday life. Even the most impressive, new, and exciting things can only be so for a little while. New turns to old; novelty turns to expectations. The city passed by as Kennedy looked steadily forward, unaware of its presence. His mind was elsewhere. He went through HeadChat messages for work. He scrolled through his Birdie feed. He used Phaneron to overlay various experiences of being elsewhere with other people.

For a brief moment, he turned everything off to look out the pod window at the city and people around him as they really were. People on the pod were laughing to themselves without anyone or anything around them. People were staring forward, blankly smiling. Out of the window, the cityscape appeared desaturated and dull; quiet and uninteresting. A horrible sense of anxiety and despair and loneliness came over Kennedy. He quickly reactivated his display screen.

Chapter 3: Incomprehension

As he approached the stop for his apartment, Kennedy received a LernaOS notification that read: *Updates Available. Do you want to restart and install these updates now?* Kennedy quickly tapped on the option reading: *Remind Me Tomorrow.* In general, there was never really an opportune time to restart, and right now was no different. He was out and about, just getting off work, feeling extra anxious and in a low mood, certainly in need of his BMI. He always planned to run the software updates when he was asleep, but he almost always forgot or didn't care enough to disrupt his nightly routine, which typically involved falling asleep while using various BMI apps.

When Kennedy got home, he lay in bed charging. While charging, he administered a nap aid through Epoché, which essentially made him just sort of lay there doing nothing—not asleep, but not awake. Just mindlessly laying there. He felt weird. He wasn't sure why he even put himself into a sleep mode. He had things he wanted to do that night. He wanted to exercise on his treadmill, read more of a book he had been meaning to finish, and do some journaling about his goals and plans for his career and future. But simultaneously, he didn't really care. Everything he needed or wanted neurochemically, he got as soon as he thought about it—often before he even knew he wanted it. While he lay there in a dazed state, he thought about himself—his hopes, his aspirations, his sense of who he was. It felt more like a memory of something than an observation. He closed his eyes and breathed in quickly.

The next morning, something must have been wrong. When Kenney woke up and opened his heads-up display screen, he couldn't seem to get into his BMI. The screen read: *Sorry, we don't recognize this person. Don't have a Lerna ID? Sign up here.* In a confused, delirious panic, Kennedy turned his display screen off and on again. The same error messaged came up: *Sorry, we don't recognize this person. Don't have a Lerna ID? Sign up here.* Kennedy's panic intensified. He forced shutdown his BMI device, holding down the button on his head for five seconds. The device deactivated from his brain, restoring it to its organic state. He felt weird and vulnerable. He hadn't really completely turned his BMI off since he got it, and now, without it, he felt like a part of him was missing. Anxiety and boredom fought in his head, smashing up against the cage of his skull.

He quickly got up and tried to calm himself down. He went over to the kitchen to get something in his system. Every morning, he had a supplement drink, which he began to prepare for himself. He immediately realized that he now had no idea what the right amount of each supplement powder was. The BMI always calculated the servings for him based on the tension in his hand and arm muscles. And since he hadn't needed to remember it in a while, and now he couldn't access his memory files, he couldn't even remember how much to manually measure out. His hand began to subtly shake, overwhelmed by this simple, mundane task.

Kennedy turned his BMI back on. When the heads-up display activated, to his immense relief, it seemed to be working. The screen read: *Would you like to save this Brain ID?* Somewhat confused, Kennedy hit *Save*. Then, he received a notification from Epoché suggesting a dose of calmness, which he eagerly accepted. He felt much better.

Chapter 3: Incomprehension

Kennedy went to work and continued about his day as normal.

After work, he walked around the city for a little while with John.

Following a long silence, Kennedy said, "Do you ever … do you ever feel like … sometimes you're just kind of observing yourself doing things, but it doesn't even feel like you? Like you're just watching things happen?"

"Yeah, kind of. I at least know what you mean, I think. There's a word for it … I don't remember what it is, though. Why? Do you?" John said.

"Kind of. Nothing crazy. Just like here and there sometimes with work or regular routine stuff. It's like I'm just doing things, and I'm not even sure why, but I just keep doing things to distract myself away from being unsure, but then I just end up even more unsure. I don't know. It's weird."

"Interesting. Yeah, I mean I just try not to think about stuff like that too much," John said.

The two walked in silence for a second.

"Are you all good, man?" John continued.

"Yeah, I'm fine."

Kennedy returned to his apartment and sat by himself at his kitchen table. He ate while using the Swap app. He was Swapping with a famous, wealthy man who often hung out with attractive women and lived (what seemed like) a luxurious, active lifestyle. Kennedy didn't really know why he did this. He didn't care about the man; he didn't even really want to be like the man; and the experience was often riddled with anxious and depressive feelings. But it was some strange, prurient curiosity that

Kennedy couldn't seem to help himself from. Suddenly, his BMI screen closed. The panic from earlier in the morning returned, increasing with each passing second. He tried reopening his display screen. It opened but then closed itself back out immediately. Then, the BMI shut itself off completely. Kennedy felt lightheaded, yet his body felt heavy. He felt like his kitchen wasn't real. It suddenly looked foreign and distant to him, like he wasn't sure what it was for. Individual objects became difficult to discern, including himself. He felt like he was almost perceiving himself in third person. He felt so anxious and alone. He felt like he didn't even have himself.

Suddenly, his BMI turned itself back on.

He immediately received a notification from Epoché suggesting a dose of pleasure, which he accepted. He felt better. He updated and reopened the Swap app and began using it again. Everything seemed to be working normally. *It must have just been the app,* Kennedy thought to himself, hastily finishing his meal.

The next morning, when Kennedy awoke, his bedroom was green. He quickly leaned up and rubbed his eyes. Everything was slower, like there was a slight lag between the actual motion of his head and eyes and what he was perceiving. He felt numb, but the numbness was somehow uncomfortable, like an emptiness that made him restless to feel something. He couldn't get out of bed. He couldn't seem to locate his thoughts well enough to instruct or perhaps convince his body to move. He almost didn't care though. It was as if the very feeling he was experiencing made him also not care about how horrible the feeling was. Apathy might be one of the

Chapter 3: Incomprehension

most dangerous states, because one of its side effects is not caring about its side effects.

After a little while, the lagging subsided, and Kennedy felt enough control over himself to shut down his BMI and get up. He kept it off while he went about his morning routine—though he soon realized it was now well into the afternoon. He had missed some work and decided to try to work from home for a while. He still had his handtop computer, which he retrieved from his closet so he could use web browsers, text chats, and other software for basic tasks. He could still connect to the Internet and had access to some of his accounts for general websites and computer-compatible applications. But without his Lerna ID, he couldn't access anything else. He couldn't access his private keys and IDs, his multi-factor authenticators, his thought and memory files, his primary way of communicating with people and conducting his work, and the plethora of BMI applications and features that he was now dependent on. The notifications, updates, and tracking; all the things he used to sustain his positive mental state, how he regulated his anxiety and depressive thoughts, calmed himself down, and so on.

Even though it had only been a relatively short time since he used his computer regularly, it was now uncomfortable to use. It was a handheld device with extendable arms and mounts. It projected a holographic keyboard out of the front and monitor screens out of the top that could all be interacted with by touch. Using it frustrated Kennedy even more than using the lagging BMI. After a couple of hours, he became so frustrated he just turned the computer off and his BMI back on.

Kennedy went to the Lerna Support page and navigated through the options: *Help charging, Help connecting, Downloading new applications, Account issues,* and *Service and repairs.* He was unsure of what was wrong, but he selected *Service and repairs.* Two subsequent options appeared: *Schedule a visit* and *Contact us.* Kennedy tapped on *Contact us.* It didn't do anything. He tapped on *Schedule a visit* instead. It brought him to another page with two more options: *Device performance* and *Repairs and physical damage.* He selected *Device performance.* More options appeared: *Device frozen or unresponsive, Unexpected shutdown or restart, Signal quality, System slowness, Battery performance, Error messages,* and *Other.* He selected *Unexpected shutdown or restart.* A video popped up and began playing. A cheery but contrived male voice began speaking over corporate stock music composed of a bubbly, upbeat tempo layered on top of a low background hum that all together somehow conveyed the emotion of no emotion at all. Kennedy impatiently watched the video as it showed him how to force shutdown his BMI, which he had already done with no success. While watching, he received a mental notification from Epoché suggesting a pleasure dose, which he eagerly accepted. The video went on to explain that his issue could be because the device had not been updated to the latest LOS, and it recommended ensuring that the device was up to date.

Kennedy promptly updated the LOS. It took around fifteen minutes and then restarted his device. Hesitantly, he opened his BMI back up and began using it. To his immense relief, everything seemed fine. *That must have been it,* he thought to himself.

Chapter 3: Incomprehension

Kennedy went to the coworking office space for the rest of the day.

As soon as he sat down at his workstation, John asked him if everything was ok.

"Hey. You there, man?" John said, poking Kennedy on the shoulder.

Kennedy snapped out of what must have been a mindless daze.

"Yeah, hey. Sorry. Yeah, everything's good." He paused for a brief moment. Then he continued, "I was just having a weird issue with my BMI this morning."

"Oh shit. What happened?!"

"I don't know. It was like not recognizing me or something the other day, and then this morning, it seemed to be like glitching and lagging."

"Jesus, man. Everything's good now, though?" John asked.

"Yeah, I think I just needed to update the sof–(({public void<doctype>meta charset=/," Kennedy said while giving John a kind of strange, deadpan look.

"Hmm. Okay, well, I'm glad you got it working, man," John said, somewhat confused, never having heard any of those code terms before. He didn't want to sound dumb, though, so he pretended like he understood. "But anyway. I was just about to head out. You coming in tomorrow?" John continued.

"Yeah, I'll be here. I'll see you tomorrow," Kennedy said with a confused look on his face.

Kennedy waited for John to get up and leave. Then, he brought up his work on his display screen. The market was up that day. Kennedy filled out several reports for clients he was working with, detailing potential opportunities in the market. While filling out a report, he thoughtlessly typed: *int fN, sN, tN; <<; cin >> {void see npc advisor. stop.}(! = 0;// Note. The following conditions set.) m_ = find key = = null ({Kill by setting value to now} << fN << + << sN << sum; return 0.*

"But anyway. I was just about to head out. You coming in tomorrow?" John asked Kennedy.

"Yeah ... see you tomorrow," Kennedy said with a confused look on his face.

He looked around. The entire coworking space was empty. It was a bit late, but the space almost always had at least a couple people working in it. Kennedy brought up work on his display screen. Suddenly, a pop-up window appeared. It was an ad. It read: *What's the point? Does anything matter? Does anyone care? Will anyone ever understand? Do you find yourself asking these sorts of questions? Existence can be hard! Live a more fulfilled life with premium beliefs and convictions!* Underneath the text was an image of a woman with her head opened up in a cartoony manner. Seeds were being dropped into it by an ominous, digital hand. Kennedy tried closing out, but he couldn't. Instead, more pop-up windows opened. One had an image of a man aggressively pointing down at a young child with his other hand holding the child's shirt collar. Text read: *Repressed memories? Childhood trauma? Extract it out with Leaks!* Kennedy tried to gain control over his thoughts, over what was being displayed to him and sent across his brain, but he couldn't. He couldn't do anything. He was helpless.

More pop-up windows came up and read: *What's the*

Chapter 3: Incomprehension

point? Does anything matter? You're not special. You're not good enough. You're not worthy. Everyone lives and dies alone. No one will ever understand you. But that's ok! Premium beliefs and convictions are as good as real ones!

What's the point anyway!?
What's the point anyway!?
What's the point anyway!?

"Everything okay?" a woman suddenly asked Kennedy with her hand placed softly on his shoulder.

Kennedy snapped out of it, and his display screen suddenly closed completely. He looked around. There were several people in the office. He looked at the woman.

"Yeah ... I'm ... I'm fine. Thank you," he replied.

"Okay. You just seemed like you were ... seemed like maybe you were having a panic attack. I know one when I see one," the woman continued in a bit of a whisper.

"Yeah. Work. You know how it is," Kennedy replied.

"Okay. Well, drinking water always helps me," the woman said before gently walking away.

Kennedy looked back around to make sure that the other people in the office space weren't looking at him. Then, he sat there for a moment trying to collect himself. He opened his display screen again and went straight to the Lerna Support page. He navigated back to where he was earlier. He skipped the video and went to the other options and information on the page. There were two articles. He read both of them. They were mostly useless—generic and vague. At the bottom of both articles, though, it said: *If you need more help, contact <u>Lerna Support here</u>*. Kennedy tapped on the text, which opened up a new page that asked him to select the problem in need of assistance. None of the categories seemed right, and Kennedy wasn't even sure what the problem was. He selected the option that seemed the closest: *Disordered thinking & functionality.* He followed the submission process. In the description box, he wrote:

> Hi,
>
> I have been experiencing several issues with my BMI. It is closing out of applications, not recognizing my account, shutting off on its own, and lagging and glitching. I have been experiencing disordered thinking and unsettling feelings as well. My device has not been damaged in anyway. I've tried forced restarting, updating the LOS, and putting it into recovery mode. Nothing has worked.
>
> Please assist.
>
> Thank you.

Kennedy submitted the form.

The next morning, he awoke to a response. It read:

> Hi Kennedy,
>
> I have reviewed your submission, and I am very sorry to hear about the issues you are experiencing. Unfortunately, without having the device, we are unable to diagnose the problem. Have you reviewed our trouble shooting videos and articles

Chapter 3: Incomprehension

on our Lerna Support page? I have provided links below. We typically recommend ensuring that your device is up to date with the latest operating system, administering a forced restart, and then entering recovery mode if you still experience a problem.

If this does not work, you can always schedule an appointment for a diagnosis, repair, or replacement under <u>Service and Repairs.</u>

<u>You can visit our Support page here.</u>

Hope this helps.

Have a great day ahead!

Thanks for using Lerna Support.

Your feedback helps us improve our service. <u>Tap here to rate our service.</u>

To contact us again about this question, reply directly to this message. For new questions, please visit <u>Lerna Support</u> or HeadCall us at <u>LernaCalls</u>.

Kennedy promptly went to the Lerna Support page to schedule an appointment. When he went to schedule an appointment, though, it stated that there was a waitlist at all locations. The earliest availability for service and repairs at any of the locations near him was twenty-two days away. He remembered the HeadCall ID in the message and went back to it. He tapped on the text reading *Lerna Calls*, which brought up the calling application on his BMI.

It rang twice, and then an automated voice answered.

"Welcome to Lerna Support. Calls are recorded for evaluation and to improve service technologies. I am an automated system. How can I help you today?"

"Emergency diagnosis ... and repair needed," Kennedy said with a frustrated yet uncertain tone in his voice.

"Got it. Thank you. Repairs and services can be scheduled through our website on the Lerna Support page under Service and Repairs. Will that be all you need assistance with today?"

"No. I need to schedule an emergency repair."

"If you are experiencing an emergency, please seek appropriate emergency assistance. Will that be all you need assistance with today?"

"Holy shit," Kennedy said with a tightness in his voice that coiled the *l* and embossed the *t*.

"I do not know how to respond to that. If you would like further assistance, please visit our Support page or submit a request through our contact forms. Will that be all you need assistance with today?"

Kennedy ended the call. He looked back through the website for other call IDs specific to each Lerna location. He was relieved to see that each location had a different ID. He tapped on the one associated with the location he originally got his BMI from.

It rang twice.

"Welcome to Lerna Support. Calls are recorded for evaluation and to improve service technologies. I am an automated system. How can I help you today?"

"I need to talk with someone!" Kennedy yelled inside his head.

"I am a fully competent processing system who can

Chapter 3: Incomprehension

understand and communicate complex inquires. What do you need assistance with today?"

"I am in need of an emergency diagnosis and repair," Kennedy said firmly.

"Got it. Thank you. Firstly, I do apologize that you're experiencing this issue. Can you please provide me with your zip code and a range that you'd be willing travel, so I can take a look at our appointment availabilities?"

"02143. I'll go pretty much anywhere."

"Got it. Thank you. Can you please provide me with a range that you'd be willing to travel?"

"Two hundred miles," Kennedy replied frustratedly.

"Got it. Thank you. One moment please."

There was a long silence. A low visceral, non-rhythmic song began playing. An up-tempo beat began playing on top of it. It seemed to add anxiety and irritation to the moment as opposed to doing what it was designed to do—comfort and fill the void.

The music cut out.

"Hi. Can you please confirm that you are still there?"

"Yes, I am still here."

"Ok. The earliest availability for any appointment in your range is in nineteen days at Point Place Facility for 3 p.m. on Tuesday, March 23. Will this work for you?"

Kennedy's bedroom suddenly went black. The voice sounded like it was behind a wall. His heart raced. The HeadCall application closed. What looked like datamoshing fragments of colors and shapes trailed across his vision.

Kennedy stayed in bed for the rest of the day. To avoid any further issues, he turned his BMI off and used his computer instead.

Using the BMI was bad, but so was not using the BMI. He was caught in a horrible paradigm in which the problem was also the solution, and the solution was also the problem.

CHAPTER 4: REHABILITATION

The next morning, Kennedy awoke to an onslaught of pop-up windows. His BMI had turned itself back on somehow. He felt a horrible mental pressure, like someone had wrapped a thousand rubber bands around his brain. He just lay there, staring at all the pop-up windows racing through his mind. *Want to die? Forget horrible memories and start fresh!* one read with an image of a half-metamorphosized baby. Another had big text that read: *Feel social without any of the hassle! Five voices in your head are better than one!* Underneath was an image of a man looking up, smiling with his mouth open, like he was talking to himself. Kennedy tried closing out of the windows, but the BMI was lagging so much, he struggled to control what he was doing. His sense of himself felt completely fragmented, like part of who he was had been lost forever. He didn't care. He continued using his BMI as if everything was fine. He used the Epoché app frequently throughout the morning, which helped make things bearable enough to continue.

After a little while, Kennedy got up out of bed and left his apartment. He skipped getting ready. He didn't brush

Chapter 4: Rehabilitation

his teeth, eat any food, or shower. He was still wearing the clothes he had slept in.

He sat on a hyperloop pod alone. The city flew by and around him. The lagging on the BMI caused the city to blur and datamosh, the buildings and people breaking apart into trailing colored, cubic pieces, all blending into one image of indiscernible nothingness. Pop-up windows overlayed on top. He just sat there.

He arrived at the Lerna facility he originally received his BMI from. It wasn't open yet. He checked the time on his display screen. It was 9:44 a.m., about fifteen minutes before the location opened. He waited out front by the entrance. He caught sight of his reflection in the side of the massive glass building. He looked closer; his nose almost pressed right up against the window. His face looked like a mass of fragments and bits of colors, shapes, and light. It was indistinct and unfamiliar.

A notification rapidly opened and closed on his display. It read: *Lerna ID not recognized.*

Lerna ID not recognized.

Lerna ID not recognized.

Suddenly, a woman walked by Kennedy and entered the building without any issue. Confused and irritated, Kennedy followed after her. He wanted to quickly catch the woman and ask her what time her appointment was to see if she was early and maybe he could try to squeeze in right before her. When he got inside, though, she was gone. The lobby of the building was completely empty with none of the display items that were there before. It was just a big empty space with cement floors and white walls, except for the chairs and obelisks that were still at the front. Kennedy went up to an obelisk.

"Kennedy Weatherly. Walk-in," he said.

The obelisk didn't do anything.

Kennedy took a seat in one of the chairs. He waited for a minute, then ten, then twenty, then an hour. He checked the time on his display screen. It was almost 11:30 a.m. Not one person had come in. Epoché prompted a notification for a dose of calmness, which he accepted.

Finally, he got up and went over to the doors at the front of the lobby. He pulled at them. To his surprise, they opened. He walked into the long hallway, and the doors closed behind him.

"Hello?" Kennedy called out, his voice echoing back to him.

No one answered. He began down the hallway, knocking on each door as he passed them. He tried opening them, but they were all locked. The hallway got darker and darker as he walked further. The darkness appeared to have a noise to it, like old video footage. At some point, the hallway became almost pitch black. Kennedy stood at the final threshold of light. He stared into the void. He felt a desire to walk into it.

Before he did, he yelled out, "Hello? Anyone?"

No one answered. He stood there for a moment.

Then, there was a sudden click. A man exited one of the rooms a few doors behind him. He wore a white lab coat and appeared to be in his twenties—about the same age as Kennedy. He looked kind of familiar. When the man noticed Kennedy, his body jolted back, and his eyes widened.

Chapter 4: Rehabilitation

"What are you doing back here?" asked the man.

"Hi, I'm ... I'm just trying to see if there are any opening for appointments today to have my BMI looked at. I'm having a problem with it, and no one's been able to help me."

"Well, there's no more appointments today," the man said before pausing for a moment, "but I'd be happy to take a look if you'd like."

Kennedy was confused but relieved.

The man walked back into the room he came out of. Kennedy followed him.

The room was almost completely empty except for a large couch and an armchair that faced each other.

The man pointed at the couch.

"Go ahead and just lay down on the couch for me."

Kennedy lied flat on his back with his head propped up on a pillow and his face pointed straight up to the ceiling.

The man sat down in the armchair opposite him.

"So, what exactly have you been experiencing?" the man asked.

"I feel like I've ... lost control of myself, or maybe I never had it all, and I'm just looking for something that isn't there. It's like I just do things mindlessly and for no real reason. I feel like everything is just pointless and in disarray, but I just keep going, keep striving, keep doing things. It's like a vague sense of hope that something will come along and make me feel connected and whole, but nothing ever comes, and the vague hope turns into a vaguer sense of self and life. I don't even really know who I am or what I am. I don't know my own thoughts from the worlds, and I don't know what's real in the world anymore."

A silence filled the room.

"I'm going to do a quick system scan if that's okay?" the man asked as he got up and walked over to where Kennedy's head was.

"Yeah, whatever you need to do."

The man took out a device and scanned Kennedy's BMI.

A few moments passed.

"Well, there doesn't appear to be any obvious hardware issues. Everything looks good in terms of the electrode arrays and their connection points. Battery's good. Housing's good. Software is up to date. My guess is that it might be an account issue. Do you have things backed up?"

"I have some stuff. But not a lot. I haven't even really been able to access certain stuff to try to back it up for a while because it just says it doesn't recognize me or won't let me."

"Okay. Well, if it is somehow a hardware issue, your options are restoring your device, and if that doesn't work, replacing your device. However, if you do either of those, anything that isn't or can't be backed up will be lost. But if it's an account issue, you can't transfer data from one Lerna ID to another. So, if you have to set up a new Lerna ID, that's even worse, depending on what you haven't backed up and need. Account issues aren't really my area, though, so I wouldn't be able to confirm one way or another what exactly is going on. I would contact the support team and explain to them what I told you and that you want your account diagnosed."

"Okay. Thank you," Kennedy said.

Chapter 4: Rehabilitation

Kennedy got up and began walking out of the room.

"Also," the man interrupted, "keep in mind you can, of course, turn off or remove the device completely. If something is causing you a problem, sometimes the best thing you can do is try to learn how to live without it instead of always trying to make it so the thing itself is less of a problem."

"Okay. Yeah, true. Thanks," Kennedy said, continuing to walk out the door.

While on the pod home, Kennedy turned his BMI off. He stared blankly out the window at the passing city—a cacophony of people whom he didn't know and would never know, each living their own lives with their own struggles, their own desires, their own needs; each so alone and bored, they drilled holes in their heads to try to escape themselves. He thought about how there was this entire world out there that, without his BMI, he couldn't access. Without his BMI, it didn't exist. It wasn't real. It was merely inside the heads of other people. But to all those people, it was more real than the *real world*. It's where all those people truly were. Kennedy reached his finger up to the top of his head and held down the button, turning his BMI back on.

Once he got home, Kennedy did as the man instructed. When he went to the Lerna Support page, though, there were no options for account issues. There was a search bar, however, which he used to search for it. An option came up that read: *Manage and use your Lerna Id.* He selected it. Several articles came up, which he quickly skimmed through. They contained nothing useful. At the bottom of the articles, there was a contact submission box, which he used to go through the same submission process he had before, but this time stating that he was in need of an account diagnosis.

The next day, Kennedy tried working from home, but the periodic lagging and glitching made it almost impossible. He stayed in bed most of the day. His bedroom, though lit brightly by the afternoon sun, was dark and narrowly perceivable. Neon colors and fragmented images filled the dark room whenever Kennedy navigated across apps or other BMI features. Apps opened and closed on their own, activating various features and effecting his mind. He just lay there, passively watching and experiencing it all.

Eventually, Kennedy felt enough guilt to outweigh the despondency, and he got up and went into the office. After trying to work for a while, he went for a short walk around the city with John. Kennedy had been fairly quiet about the progression of the whole issue, feeling weird and embarrassed by it. John was vaguely aware, but he only really understood the surface level.

As the two walked along the city street, the sun setting behind them, John asked Kennedy, "So, are you just going to get a new one if you can't figure anything else out?"

"I really hope it doesn't come to that, but yeah, I suppose," Kennedy replied. "I still have an appointment scheduled in a couple weeks. So, if all else fails, hopefully it is a hardware issue, and a new BMI will solve it. But I'll still lose so much shit. So much of what I have is locked up in my BMI right now that I can't even transfer or get to to back up."

Chapter 4: Rehabilitation

"Fuck. Like what?"

"Memory files, application settings, contacts, Epoché preferences and mental tracking data, and all the stuff you can't even really backup. Just like general settings, passwords, codes, IDs. Everything."

"Holy shit. Fuck. I'm sorry, man. How are you ... how are you doing?"

"I mean, I feel fucked."

"Yeah, I'm sorry you have to deal with this. It's scary how we can become so dependent on this stuff, and it can all just be taken away without any real explanation. It's like we create the need for things we don't even need just to eventually lose them."

The two paused for a moment.

"Yeah, everything is way more complicated than it seems. It's like there are a million little threads attached to everything—everything you think and choose and encounter—and all the threads are destined to get tangled up eventually. But at that point, you can't even really see the individual threads anymore. It's just a giant knot. And even if you could pin-point the threads that are causing you a problem, you can't even get to them to pull them out."

CHAPTER 5: DISCONSOLATION

Kennedy spent days going back through the same process he had already gone through—contacting Lerna Support, trying to explain what he was experiencing, being passed off onto somebody else, so on and so forth. Nobody seemed to know what the problem was. Each person Kennedy talked to had their specific role with their specific responsibilities. If they didn't understand the problem, they passed him off to somebody else who might; if the next person didn't, the process continued.

As more time went by, Kennedy's problem only got worse. He continued to struggle to get out of bed. He felt more and more tired and lethargic throughout the day. The world seemed to be almost glazed over with an increasingly thick, opaque sludge. He was confused and scared, yet numb and indifferent. His BMI continued to glitch and have problems, though he continued to use it as much as he could. He needed it to help him deal with the very problems it was causing.

After several days and many back-and-forth conversations with different members of the Lerna Support team,

Chapter 5: Disconsolation

Kennedy received a message from a Lerna Support supervisor. The message read:

> Hi Kennedy,
>
> I have been informed about your issue. I understand that account problems can be extremely frustrating. However, we were unable to find any issues with your account. Of course, we are unable to provide any assistance to unknown problems.
>
> You can setup a new account on the Lerna website. Any previous account information, settings, memories, applications, and data that cannot be accessed elsewhere will unfortunately be lost.
>
> Hope this helps.
>
> Thank you,
> Martin L.

Kennedy immediately replied:

> Hi Martin,
>
> It does not help. I am confused as to why nobody can help me. I have been told that it is not a hardware problem, it is not a software problem, and it is not an account problem. What else is there?
>
> No one seems to be able to clarify what the issue might be, let alone help. My entire life is

associated with my current Lerna ID. It is my life at this point. Can you please refer me to the person above you?

Thank you,
Kennedy

Two more days went by. Kennedy received another response. It read:

Hi Kennedy,

This is Alicia, a supervisor at <u>Lerna Support</u>.

Unfortunately, we are unable to go around the processes we have in place. While there's no current solution to your problem, we appreciate you taking the time to share and let us know what you are looking for. Most of the improvements we make come from suggestions by customers like you.

Let me know if you have any other concerns.

Thank you,
Alicia L.

Kennedy's head vibrated, and his chest knotted. He felt lost at sea—a casualty of society's rip current.

A couple more weeks went by. It was the day of the appointment that Kennedy had made for a service and

Chapter 5: Disconsolation

repair, which he had since changed to be an upgrade and replacement.

He went to the Lerna facility, went through the same process, and sat waiting in the same lobby. When his name was called, he walked into the same long hall and then into one of the procedure rooms.

He sat in the surgical chair in the middle of the room as the helmet-like half-dome machine moved over his head and began scanning his brain. He took the three conscious sedation tablets but couldn't really tell the difference between how he felt before or after.

"Please lay back, keep your head straight, and stay as still as possible," the automated voice said.

The helmet-like device began removing his existing BMI, extracting each thread and electrode from his brain. Then, it implanted the new model. Around thirty minutes later, the procedure was complete.

"Congratulations. You are now fully integrated with your new Lerna BMI 8Z. Your device is already registered and synced with your existing Lerna ID. If you experience any issues or complications, please visit Lerna Support for additional assistance. Thank you, and have a wonderful day."

Kennedy sat on a pod on his way back to his apartment. Hesitantly, he reached up and held the button down on the top of his head. The display screen appeared. His Lerna ID was already logged in. A good portion of what he needed was there—his contacts, his apps, a portion of his memory files, some of his security details and account information. There was enough there for Kennedy to let out a giant sigh of relief as he laid back in the pod seat. It was over now. Everything was going to be ok

Suddenly, Kennedy was back in his apartment. He had no memory of arriving or walking in. He was sitting on his couch, slouched back. The room was dark, with a pink and green hue and thin vertical lines covering everything. A message on his display screen read: *Sorry, we don't recognize this person. Don't have a Lerna ID? Sign up here.*

"Fuck! Fuck! Fuck!" Kennedy cried out with tears in his eyes and hands full of his hair.

He tapped on *Sign up here*, which brought him to the Lerna ID setup screen. In a frenzy of desperation and rage, he haphazardly created a new Lerna ID. Then, he set up a new Brain ID.

After essentially starting everything over, somehow, inexplicably, the same problems just continued happening. Error messages started popping up, and subtle glitches and lags began to occur.

Kennedy ran out of his apartment and took the hyperloop track that went two thousand miles to where the Lerna headquarters was located.

When he arrived, he walked up to the building—a massive tube-shaped structure covered in dark glass and spiraling metal beams. It almost looked alive, like a serpent. It was so large, Kennedy couldn't see where it ended.

There appeared to be no door. He walked along the side of the building looking for one, passing glass pane after glass pane, like scales of skin. After fifteen minutes passed, Kennedy finally reached what appeared to be one

Chapter 5: Disconsolation

of the ends of the building. He couldn't tell if it was the front or the back or neither. There was a large circular door made of two vertical pieces of glass. He approached it and cupped his hands around his eyes against it to look inside. Suddenly, the lower portion of the door opened. He walked in.

Inside, there was a large, circular room with a long, massive hallway extending off of it. There were no other doors, no signs, no people—nothing.

"Hello!?" Kennedy said, his voice echoing down the hallway.

No one answered.

He started walking. Soon, he encountered multiple other hallways branching off the main one. They too apparently lead to more long, sprawling hallways, each with more hard corners leading to even more hallways. There was nothing in any of them. No doors, no rooms, nothing. The hallways were hot, and there was a low but noticeable hum echoing throughout them. The walls seemed to almost throb; the ceiling lights seemed to pulse. A pop-up window appeared on Kennedy's display. It read: *Let's face it. You're useless. How about a subconscious sense of purpose?* Kennedy closed the window out and kept walking down the halls—a bit faster now. He had no idea where he was going, and after not too long, he had no idea where he had come from. Another pop-up window appeared. It was an image of a man standing in a dark alley way. He was backlit, but you could kind of see his face. He had an exaggerated, cartoonish frown. Large text read: *Stay.* Smaller text underneath read: *Every 20 seconds, someone dies by suicide. There's always light at the end of the tunnel.* Kennedy started to run. The hallways became a blur of darkness with no end in sight. He ran faster and faster. He didn't know why he was running. It was only causing him to become more lost.

Eventually, he stopped. He turned around and tried to retrace his steps but couldn't find his way out. He rounded corner after corner, until suddenly, he saw what appeared to be a source of light in the distance. He walked toward it and soon found himself in an open office space filled with people sitting at tables and desks with trees and plants scattered around them. The space was warm and bright but artificially so. A woman sat at a desk at the front. Further back in the office, there was a large, glass, ornate, cubical room. There was a woman sitting inside it. Kennedy recognized her. It was the CEO.

"Can I help you, sir?" the woman at the front desk said.

Kennedy moved his eyes from the woman in the back to the woman at the desk.

"Um. Hi. Yeah ... I need ... I need help."

"Okay. Do you have an appointment?"

"No. I need to speak with ..." Kennedy paused and looked at the CEO, "... her," he said, pointing at the CEO.

"Well, if you don't have an appointment, I'm afraid you'll have to leave and return when you do."

Kennedy stared at the woman. His face took on a disturbed, destitute look—his face muscles tightening, his cheek bones pulsating, his eyes widening. She was his last hope. Everyone in the space suddenly froze. In a jolt, Kennedy jumped over the desk and charged toward the

Chapter 5: Disconsolation

glass office in the back. Everything began moving again with a lurching glitch. The office space fragmented with strange colors and lines. The people in the office suddenly appeared startled. After only a few strides, two sets of robotic arms extruded down from the ceiling and restrained Kennedy by his arms and shoulders.

"Please! Please! I just need help! I just need help!" He yelled, his face clenching even tighter as if he were now crying but without tears.

The CEO observed the scene from the glass office. She held still for a moment, staring intently at Kennedy. Then, the robotic arms let him go. The glass doors to her office slid open, and she nodded at him as if gesturing Kennedy in.

He walked slowly into the office. The robot arms followed over him.

"Hi. I ... I just need help. No one ... No one's been able to help me," Kennedy said to the CEO.

"Have a seat," she replied.

Kennedy took a seat in a chair opposite her. The doors closed behind him.

"And what makes you think I can help you?" the woman continued.

"Well ... aren't you the CEO? Don't you run everything?"

The woman let out a soft but noticeable exhale as she smiled with her lips clenched together.

"You know that whole maze of hallways you just came through?"

"Yeah," Kennedy replied with a shakiness to his voice.

"All of that, this whole building, is one giant data

center. A self-sustaining infrastructure of algorithms and code and processes run on servers, storage subsystems, networking switches, routers, firewalls, and everything else that I couldn't even tell you about. I don't even really know how most of it works. That's the job of those who I'm assuming you've probably already spoken with. But the truth is, Kennedy, those who are assigned to help you in the maze are themselves also in the maze. No one ever really knows what's going on. By the time they do, things have likely already changed, and it's no longer even relevant. New problems. New uncertainties. So on and so forth. No one runs everything. Barely anybody runs anything. Just their little piece of the puzzle, unable to ever see what image the puzzle is creating."

"But it's your device that's causing me a problem. Someone must know how solve it," Kennedy said.

"Our technology solves a lot of problems for people, but we can't always solve all the problems our technology causes. That's for another company and another technology. The maze just continues."

Kennedy stared blankly back at the woman, holding still for a moment. Then, he ran back out into the open office area and toward a group of employees.

He yelled at them, "Please! I need help. Can any of you ... Can any of you help me?! I just need help ... I just need help with my BMI."

The employees stared blankly back at Kennedy. No one said or did anything. Kennedy's body collapsed underneath him as he broke down crying. The robot arms had already restrained him again, and they now held him up and began carrying him off.

Chapter 5: Disconsolation

After he settled down a bit, the robot arms hovered over him as he walked back through the maze of hallways. He observed the light from the office space fade behind him with harsh light flairs filling his peripherals until the halls turned back to darkness. There was no more light.

After taking the pod home, Kennedy sat at his kitchen table, alone, staring forward. He looked lifeless, like all the muscles in his face had given up trying to hold an expression.

After sitting at the table for a while, he got up and went into one of the drawers in his kitchen. He retrieved a screwdriver. He walked back to the kitchen table and sat down. He put the screwdriver on the table and stared at it for a moment. Then, he took it. He raised it up to the top of his head. He pressed down and around in a circular motion, simultaneously rotating it up and down. Then, he reached up and pulled the BMI out from his head. It dropped onto the table in front of him, covered in blood and thousands of threads once connected to every little thought and decision he made. His open skull began to bleed out. He just sat there. Then, his head and neck fell forward, smacking the table.

He was free.

ABOUT THE AUTHOR

Robert Pantano is the creator of the YouTube channel and production house known as Pursuit of Wonder, which covers similar topics of philosophy, science, and literature through short stories, guided experiences, video essays, and more.

youtube.com/pursuitofwonder
pursuitofwonder.com

Printed in Great Britain
by Amazon